Caeli's Trip

Caeli was spending the weekend with her grandmother, in a small town in Florida.

You and I have a lot of catching up to do, I have missed you grandma.

"How's school going for you?"

"It's been going great."

"How are your grades doing?"

"I've been getting A's."

"Are you going to be on the honor roll?"

"Yes, I am.

Later on, this afternoon we're going to go on a trip together.

"Are you going to tell me where we're going, or are you going to surprise me?"

"I'm going to surprise you."

"Will we be able to get ice cream there?"

"Yes," we will.

You won't be bored where we're going, and I'll be able to see a good friend of mine who works there.

We've been friends for so many years.

When we were teenagers we used to go shopping together.

Then we would go out to a restaurant for dinner.

In the end, if you can count your friends on your hand you've done pretty well.

I haven't heard you say that in a long time, that's because I forgot all about that saying.

"How comes you can't remember some things?"

"That's because my mind is aging."

"What does aging mean?"

It means that you're getting old. I like when you teach me new words, it makes me feel happy inside.

"Do you remember when you and I were looking for lightning bugs?"

"Yes," I do how could I forget.

You told me to put it in a jar, but after a short time I left it go free because I felt bad for it.

Then her grandfather walked into the room, I could hear the both of you talking in my room.

I just love it when the two of you are talking.

I left an orange soda for you, that's my favorite.

I can still remember when I used to pull you around in the wagon, around the block.

"Yes," I do.

Her grandmother noticed that the side door was open, I swear that your grandfather lives' in a barn.

I was just letting some air in here, soon there will be flies in here.

Your grandfather and I are going to get some provisions before we go on our trip.

Caeli was so excited, that she couldn't stay still.

You can get in the car awhile if you'd like, no that's alright.

Her grandmother accidentally dropped a bottle of water, and Caeli picked it up and handed it to her.

Sometime later they got on the road, Caeli was strapped into the car seat.

"Why have we stopped?"

"Your grandfather forgot to get gas"

"Are you going to pump the gas?"

"No," your grandfather does that.

An SUV pulled into the pump next to them, there was a kayak strapped to the top of it.

Suddenly the door opened to the SUV, and a Labrador retriever jumped out.

Caeli pointed to the dog that was outside, her grandmother saw her pointing.

Your grandfather and I were talking about getting a dog, but at this stage of the game it wouldn't be worth it.

I wish I could pet that dog; you don't know if it's friendly or not.

I thought that all dogs were friendly, no they aren't.

"Do you think the dog greeted grandpa?"

"I'm sure that it did."

Her grandfather came walking back to the car, he was holding a bottle of water and two rice Krispie treats.

He looked over and saw that the dog was still running around the gas station, so he went back into the station.

The man behind the counter casually looked over at him, he began asking me around who has a dog.

There was a fellow standing in the back of the store, who looked over.

He raised his hand and said yes that's my
dog.

The dog got out of your car and it's
wandering around, thanks for letting me
know.

I just didn't want to see anything happen to
it.

You have a good day now.

Just as he was opening the door to go out, a
man came out yelling I won the lottery.

You scared me, I'm sorry I'm just overly
excited.

Just as he was getting in the car, a police car
pulled in.

The man with the dog, just isn't very responsible.

I'm sure that he's probably going to get a fine, I can't believe that he still hasn't come out of the store yet.

"What are the both of you talking about?"

"We're talking about the owner of the dog."

They got back on the road; several motorcycles went past them.

Caeli was looking out the window, and a fly flew in the open window.

Rather than tell anyone about it she just sat there.

Her grandmother happened to look back at her, there's a fly flying around Caeli.

It'll probably fly out the window soon, when she saw the rice crispy treats her eyes lit up.

They were my favorite too when I was a kid.

They passed by a broken-down car on the side of the road.

This road were on is awfully winding, we're never on it for very long.

They pulled into the parking lot; this place is usually crowded by this time of day. This is

going to be a great day at the lake, I'll go
pick out a picnic table.

I can still remember this lake before it had
tables, and the dock wasn't even there.

Caeli took off her seat belt, among the other
straps and quickly got out.

She ran over to where her grandmother was,
it felt like we were in the car all day.

Her grandfather was skipping rocks across
the water, he's always liked doing that as
long as I've known him.

He taught me how to do that, it took me
many attempts.

"What do you think lives in that
lake?"

"Some fish."

"How about turtles?"

"No," I haven't seen any of them here.

I'll tell you a little story while he's doing that, about 40 years ago he went on a fishing expedition.

He caught so many fish that he didn't know what to do with all of them.

Sometime when you and him are talking one-on-one, ask him about it.

Her grandmother looked down at her watch, they should be arriving soon.

"Who will be arriving soon?"

"I can't tell you or that would ruin the surprise."

Her grandmother pointed to a patch of grass, that's where we're going to do the exercises.

It really rained yesterday and the grass is wet, don't sit down in it.

Your grandfather is bringing folding chairs over here, just be patient with him.

You look like you're struggling carrying that chair, I'm doing just fine.

Eventually they brought out all the chairs and sat in them.

Caeli was watching the birds flying over, it seemed to keep her content for a short while.

Two trucks with big trailers came rolling in, the people gathered their things from the trailer and came over to them.

Caeli was watching two people: who we're gathering something up out of the truck.

Both people were holding 2 adorable Labrador retriever puppies, carefully petting them.

They carefully put them down on the green grass, the puppies immediately intermingled with one another.

Caeli was smiling ear to ear, she got down on the grass with them.

They began giving her kisses, and before she knew it they were all climbing up all over her.

This made her grandfather so emotional that the tears began to roll down his wrinkled cheeks.

While her grandmother just sat back taking everything in.

One of the people asked is everyone ready to begin, everyone nodded yes.

The trainer was sitting in the grass Indian style, I'm going to teach all of you different yoga positions.

I'm not sure if your grandfather will be doing this, he shook his head no at her.

Maybe they can do a yoga position that's easy for him, there's no yoga position that would be good for him.

While everyone is doing yoga, there will be puppies climbing all over them.

Once there're done doing the adult yoga, they will show you how to do child yoga.

The people were giggling as the puppies were climbing up on their backs.

Your grandfather looks so forlorned, then one of the puppies ran over to him.

He carefully climbed up his leg, then a smile came on his face.

Hello little guy, I wonder what your name is.

It began pawing at him, yes you're good boy.

Caeli closed her eyes, and when she opened them, there was a puppy licking her face.

She petted the puppy on its head, and it left out a yawn.

It looks like you're putting that puppy to sleep, it's the same thing that my parents dog does.

The trainer wrapped up the adult poses, she walked over to Caeli.

My name is Caeli, it's nice to meet you.

Since this is your first time, I'm going to
instruct you through the children poses.

"Will I have to do a somersault?"

"No," you won't.

Yoga is supposed to be easy on the body and
align your energy chakras.

I've never heard that word before, you're
doing it right.

Just lean over further, bring your back leg
back further.

Take a deep breath and allow your body to
relax.

You're doing well, just keep it up, now take a rest.

I don't want to tire you out too much, so I'm just going to show you one more pose.

Stand back up, now I want you to balance on one leg, while holding your arm up.

Some of the children that I have worked with, can't do this pose, because they would easily get off balance.

You're doing well for a beginner, try to raise up your other arm.

Nice job holding up your arms, we're done with this pose now.

I see that your grandparents are having a good time over there with the puppies.

I'm booked for the next 5 weekends; this puppy yoga is catching on.

My son is actually your age, him and I do yoga everyday together.

"Have you ever swam in the lake?"

"No," my parents and grandparents tell me not to do that.

"Do these puppies all belong to you?"

"No," they live on a big farm.

It's called Puppy Haven; I've heard of that place before.

I'm lucky enough to be able to go there, there are so many dogs there.

You wouldn't know which one to pet first.

I'm sure if you would ask your grandparents nicely, they would take you there sometime.

It was nice talking to you, I'm going to have a word with your grandparents.

All the puppies were lying beside one another in the middle of the grass patch.

The people grabbed the puppies, and gently placed them down on the back seat.

The trainer waved goodbye to her, as she walked back towards the truck.

Those were the best-behaved puppies, I thought that your grandfather was going to dose off.

After quite some time everything was packed up in the back of the car, and they were making their way back to the car.

"Can I have that rice Krispie treat now?"

"Yes," you may.

Then I want you to drink some water.

2 hours later they arrived back at home.

That was the best trip ever to the lake.